The
Better
Best
Birthday

LIZZY JUDGE

To: _____

With love from:

_____

Long ago
When you turned
two

It was the best number
You ever knew

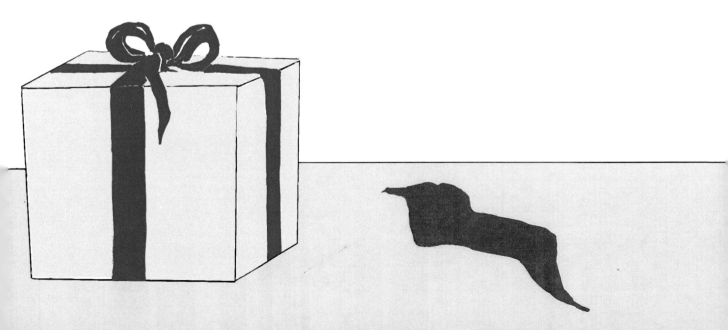

The number two
beat all the rest

But now
you're **three** -
that's better best!

What makes **three**
so cool, so great?

Turn the page,
no need to wait!

Above us the moon, stars
and sun

Three shining lights for everyone

Colors **three** - red, yellow, and blue

Make every color you ever knew

They say good things come in **threes**

Tricycles, bears, and triangular cheese!

Into the **three** bears'
cottage, did Goldilocks
barge,

Ate **three** bowls of
porridge -

Small, medium and large!

Three sides to a pizza slice

Keep away from three blind mice!

What does a table need
To stand up tall?

At least **three** legs, or

BANG, SMASH, FALL!

The crowd cheers and calls your name

Three goals - a hat trick wins the game

1   2   3

Pyramids built along the Nile

Save Mummy from the crocodile!

Stands Neptune grand,
Trident in hand

Ruling the seas
Below the land

Cars, trucks, bikes
always dashing

Red - Yellow - Green
or they'll be crashing!

On your marks,
ready - set - go!

Faster than they'll ever know

Three cheers for you -
Hip, hip, hooray!

Three is really great
It's your age today!

Don't forget about us!

The End

Coloring Pages

Made in United States
North Haven, CT
03 June 2022

19814462R00024